W9-CCD-277

TEN HISPANIC AMERICAN AUTHORS

The *Collective Biographies* Series

Collective Biographies

TEN HISPANIC AMERICAN AUTHORS

Christine M. Hill

Enslow Publishers, Inc.

40 Industrial Road   PO Box 38
Box 398   Aldershot
Berkeley Heights, NJ 07922   Hants GU12 6BP
USA   UK

http://www.enslow.com

Library of Congress Cataloging-in-Publication Data

Hill, Christine M.
    Ten Hispanic American authors / Christine M. Hill.
        p. cm. — (Collective biographies)
    Includes bibliographical references and index.
    ISBN 0-7660-1541-6 (hardcover)
    1. Hispanic American authors—Biography—Juvenile literature. 2.
Authors, American—20th century—Biography—Juvenile literature. [1.
Authors, American. 2. Hispanic Americans—Biography.] I. Title. II.
Series.
PS153.H56 H54 2001
810.9'868073—dc21   2001000307

Printed in the United States of America

10 9 8 7 6 5 4 3 2

To Our Readers:
We have done our best to make sure all Internet addresses in this book were active and
appropriate when we went to press. However, the author and the publisher have no
control over and assume no liability for the material available on those Internet sites
or on other Web sites they may link to. Any comments or suggestions can be sent by
e-mail to comments@enslow.com or to the address on the back cover.

Contents

Acknowledgments

Many thanks to the authors, who reviewed their chapters and contributed personal photographs.

Preface

How does a writer grow? I asked this question while researching and writing my previous book, *Ten Terrific Authors for Teens.* I found that the authors profiled in that book almost invariably had two things in common: They grew up loving to read, and they had family members who read aloud to them or told them stories.

You will find as you read about the Hispanic-American authors in this book that the recipe for growing as a writer remains the same. All ten of them were ardent readers. While reading aloud in their families was uncommon, most of them heard expert storytellers around their kitchen tables. Rudolfo Anaya's grandfather and Judith Ortiz Cofer's grandmother were gifted storytellers. Oscar Hijuelos and Piri Thomas both grew up listening to their mothers tell stories of their girlhoods in Cuba and Puerto Rico. Everyone Julia Alvarez knew told stories. "We didn't have TV. We didn't have books," she says. "[Storytelling] was just what people did."[1]

With the exception of Julia Alvarez, a doctor's daughter, these writers grew up in modest to very poor families. Few of them owned books. Gary Soto remembers having only three books in his house growing up. In Sandra Cisneros's home, there were no books at all. Until her mother traded coupons she'd saved for a Bible, Cisneros had not known that individuals could own books. She'd thought that books were reserved for libraries.

For youngsters who disliked school, like Nicholasa Mohr, Gary Soto, and Piri Thomas, the library was the place where they kept their love of reading alive. In fourth grade, Richard Rodriguez set himself the goal of reading all the "important books" he could find in the library. Esmeralda Santiago learned English using the alphabet books at the Brooklyn Public Library. Although Oscar Hijuelos used the New York Public Library, his favorite reading was comic books. Esmeralda Santiago also pored over comics, studying Archie and his friends to learn how to behave as an American teenager.

Interestingly, a third source of inspiration was poetry. Several of these writers grew up with family members who wrote and liked to recite poetry. Julia Alvarez's grandfather loved poetry and had a large store of it committed to memory. Judith Ortiz Cofer's grandfather wrote and recited his own poetry, as did Oscar Hijuelos's mother. Esmeralda Santiago had a poetry-writing father.

So it seems that influences like reading and storytelling and poetry help writers grow regardless of culture. But the Hispanic-American writers in this books share other and different influences from their Anglo, or English-speaking, counterparts. Most important are their complex relationships with the

Spanish and English languages and with Hispanic and American cultures.

Except for Gary Soto, the birth language of all these writers was Spanish. Six of them spoke only Spanish until they entered school.

For some, the switch to English was traumatic. Oscar Hijuelos lost his ability to speak Spanish when he was hospitalized for over a year as a preschooler. Richard Rodriguez's devout Catholic parents obeyed the request of the nuns who taught him, to speak only English at home to improve his school performance. Others moved casually and with ease from one language to the other, even within the household. Nicholasa Mohr spoke Spanish to her parents and English to her brothers. Sandra Cisneros spoke Spanish to her father and English to her mother.

Richard Rodriguez has written that an educated person must leave the family culture behind to embrace the culture of an American education. Judith Ortiz Cofer, for one, strongly disagrees. "You can and must find a channel that takes you back and forth between cultures," she says.[2] Most of these authors, however, revel in their bi-culturalism, finding that it greatly enriches their lives and writing.

Some of them, like Sandra Cisneros and Gary Soto, have become spokespersons for Hispanic-American arts and literature. Others, like Rudolfo Anaya and Oscar Hijuelos, have quietly mentored young writers behind the scenes. Some, like Esmeralda Santiago and Piri Thomas, are proud to serve as role models. In contrast, Richard Rodriguez has consciously rejected such a role.

Hispanic-American literature in English, as a whole, dates back less than fifty years. As a result, many of these writers have scored firsts. Oscar Hijuelos was the first Hispanic author to win the Pulitzer Prize for fiction. Rudolfo Anaya is considered the father of the Chicano novel, "Piri Thomas is a legend in his community."[3] It is my hope that these biographical sketches will inspire readers to seek out the work of these wonderful writers.

A Note on Names

"Hispanics don't exist," reads the headline of an article on Latino subcultures in the United States, which appeared in *U.S. News and World Report* magazine.[4] In fact, the term Hispanic American is one invented by the Anglo majority to describe Spanish-speaking Americans and their descendants. It can encompass people from four continents: Spain-Europe; the Philippines-Asia; and North and South America. As the author Linda Robinson points out, many Hispanic Americans reject the label.[5] Some wish to be referred to by their country of origin. Others, Sandra Cisneros for one, will answer only to the term "Latino," which refers to New-World Hispanics.

The point of the article is that Hispanic Americans are not all the same. Though they have the Spanish language in common, their subcultures can be very different, and they do not necessarily identify with one another.

Some Hispanic Americans form their surnames in the Spanish tradition. They use a double surname, with the father's name followed by the mother's. For example, Sandra Cisneros's father was named Alfredo Cisneros del Moral. His father's surname, Cisneros, which appears to be a middle name, is the one he passed on to his American-born children.

In some Hispanic cultures, children do not call adults Mr. or Mrs., or even Señor or Señora. Instead, they are called Don or Doña, followed by a first name. In cases where the authors in this book refer to their parents this way in their autobiographical writings, I have followed their lead. Otherwise, I refer to them in the American style.

Julia Alvarez

Julia Alvarez

(March 27, 1950–   )

"Spick! Spick! Go back to where you came from!"[1] A pack of New York City schoolboys hurled stones at ten-year-old Julia Alvarez along with their hurtful words. She didn't understand everything they said, "but I knew it couldn't be anything good from the ugly looks on their faces," she remembers.[2] They mimicked her halting English, her Spanish accent. They chorused the Chiquita Banana song. Finally, a nearby teacher stopped the abuse.

"Looking back," she says, "I can see that my path as a writer began in that playground."[3] She realized at that moment what power words held. She determined to learn English so well that Americans would sit up and take notice.

Little did those boys realize that Julia was actually a native New Yorker. She was born there on March

27, 1950, while her father was in exile in the United States. The second of four daughters, Julia soon moved with her family back to their native Dominican Republic.

The Alvarez family lived in the capital city of Santo Domingo, then called Ciudad Trujillo. Their house was next door to her mother's well-to-do extended family, the Tavareses. In summer all the relatives moved together to a beachfront cottage. Julia remembers an enchanted childhood. She grew up surrounded by luxuriant flowers and, "the smell of mangoes and the iridescent, vibrating green of hummingbirds."[4]

Her grandfather, a United Nations cultural attaché, loved to recite poetry aloud. Julia had a remarkable ability to memorize poems she heard him recite only once or twice. Her parents often called on her to perform a recitation at family gatherings.

And everyone told stories. "We didn't have TV, we didn't have books," says Alvarez. "[Storytelling] was just what people did."[5]

In 1960 ten-year-old Julia and her family fled the Dominican Republic one step ahead of the secret police. Doctor Alvarez had involved himself in a plot to overthrow the Dominican dictator, Rafael Trujillo. The family settled in a small New York apartment while Doctor Alvarez re-established his eligibility to practice medicine in the United States. Once licensed, he started a clinic in a Hispanic Brooklyn neighborhood. The Alvarezes saved money and bought a house in Queens. Their four daughters attended Catholic school.

At first, Julia struggled. "I [had] lost almost everything: a homeland, a language, family connections, a way of understanding, a warmth," she says.[6] Though she had attended an American-style school in the Dominican Republic, Julia had been a cutup and class clown. Her grades had been poor.

In America, she changed. "Coming to this country I discovered books," she says. She studied English words, examining them like treasures. "Why is it that word and not another?" she would wonder.[7] Julia spoke English at school, Spanish at home, and "Spanglish," or a mixture of the two, with her sisters.

Perceptive teachers encouraged Julia to write about her island girlhood. By the time she entered high school, she knew she would be a writer. "Writing

Julia Alvarez and her family fled the Dominican Republic after her father was involved in a plot to overthrow the Dominican dictator, Rafael Trujillo.

[became] the one place where I felt I belonged and could make sense of myself," she remembers.[8]

For high school, the Alvarez sisters won scholarships to the New England boarding school their mother had attended. Julia followed this with two years at Connecticut College, in New London, Connecticut. Two years in a row, she won the school's poetry prize. A summer spent at the prestigious Bread loaf Writers' Conference in Middlebury, Vermont, led her to transfer to nearby Middlebury College. She graduated in 1971 with highest honors. After a brief period working as a magazine editor, Alvarez entered a Master of Arts program in creative writing at Syracuse University, Syracuse, New York. She received her degree in 1975.

Then began her years as a "migrant poet," she jokes.[9] She took a variety of teaching and visiting writer positions all over the country. She wanted a job that would support her, at least barely, and give her time to write. She tooled from town to town with her belongings heaped into an old Volkswagen Beetle so rusty that the pavement showed through the floor.

During one period, she spent two years in Kentucky as a traveling poet-in-residence for the state arts commission. She gave poetry readings and workshops. She spoke in schools, prisons, nursing homes, and convents. In one small town, a grizzled farmer turned up looking for the "lady with the government." He'd heard she was in town to talk about "poultry." Alvarez explained that her mission was "poetry," not "poultry." He stayed to dictate a poem to her, since he had never learned to read or write.[10]

Alvarez also married and divorced twice in her twenties. Both marriages were short-lived. During both, she nearly gave up writing, abandoning her "heart's desire," she says.[11] Her family despaired of her settling domestically or professionally.

Finally, in her thirties, Alvarez began to find her "voice." It was an American voice with a Spanish lilt. She realized that, read out loud, her English-language writing had the rhythm and rolling sentences of her native tongue. After years of feeling torn between the two cultures, she felt that "that complexity, that richness" was exactly what inspired her.[12]

Her first poetry collection, *Homecoming*, was published in 1984, when she was thirty-three. "It was scary," she says. "Poetry is . . . so naked."[13] She worried about embarrassing her family with personal revelations. Yet she turned to personal matters when she began to write fiction. All through the 1980s, she struggled with a set of interrelated short stories about four Dominican-American sisters.

Alvarez finally put down roots in Vermont during the 1980s. She became a faculty member at Middlebury College in 1985. She also married again, in 1989. Her husband, Bill Eichner, a divorced opthamologist with two grown daughters is wholly supportive of her writing.

Her book of interrelated stories, *How the Garcia Girls Lost Their Accents*, was published in 1991 and became a best-seller. Alvarez explains that, like any writer, she uses the raw material of her experiences to create her fiction. "This distinction has not always been clear" to her family, she writes.[14] Some relatives would "correct" her accounts of true family stories, which she had fictionalized. Others would "remember" incidents that she had completely invented.

Her second novel, *In the Time of the Butterflies*, was published in 1994. It is based on the true story of four Dominican sisters who were killed for resisting the Trujillo dictatorship. Alvarez's mother, who had difficulties with the more personal *Garcia Girls*, was won over. "I'm so proud of you for writing this book," she told her grateful daughter.[15]

In the mid-1990s, Alvarez gave up teaching at Middlebury College to write full-time. She has published prolifically since then: a poetry collection, *The Other Side*, in 1995; a novel, *Yo!*, in 1997; an essay collection, *Something to Declare*, in 1998; historical novel, *In the Name of Salome*, in 2000; and a young people's novel and picture book in 2001.

Alvarez and her husband spend time yearly in the Dominican Republic. Yet she returns to the isolation of Vermont to write. She feels that splitting her time between both locations best feeds her creativity. "When I go back to the real place[,] sparks jump between that place and the place in my head," she says. "The mixture is often a clash . . . but my eye sees certain things because I'm that mixture. And the things that I see . . . are what I'll write about."[16]

Rudolfo Anaya
(October 30, 1937–   )

Baby Rudolfo sat on a soft sheepskin. His parents placed several objects within his reach. The one he picked would mark his destiny, they believed. His father, Martín, placed a saddle before him. It symbolized the *vaquero*, or cowboy, tradition of the Anayas. Other objects represented the farming tradition of his mother's Mares family. Then his mother Rafaelita, who had always longed for an education, added a paper and pencil to the choices. The baby reached for them.

When asked to describe his roots, Rudolfo Anaya looks at his feet. "I see the roots of my soul grasping the earth," he says.[1] Unlike the other writers in this book, he is neither an immigrant, nor the child or grandchild of immigrants. Instead, his ancestors have lived in New Mexico for centuries, since before it was

Rudolfo Anaya

part of the United States. He, too, has lived there all his life.

Rudolfo was born in Pastura, New Mexico, on October 30, 1937. Months after he was born, his family moved to the nearby town of Santa Rosa. Their small house stood on a cliff looking down on the Pecos River. The *llanos*, or plains, of eastern New Mexico form a beautiful, but harsh, environment. Sandstorms raged in summer and snowstorms in winter, Anaya says, while year-round "the wind blows and makes its music."[2]

Both his parents had been married before and widowed. Their household now included his mother's two children from her first marriage, as well as the couple's own seven children. Rudolfo's family and everyone he knew spoke Spanish. "As far as I knew all the world spoke Spanish," he says.[3]

"I was always in a milieu of words," Rudolfo remembers.[4] The village was close-knit, with much visiting among families. As the men played cards and dominoes around the table, they told stories, asked riddles, and recounted wise sayings. Rudolfo and the other children listened.

Grandfather Mares was a fine storyteller. Rudolfo recalls the puzzle his grandfather asked the children one night under the stars:

"There is a man with so much money
He cannot count it.
A woman with a bedspread so large
She cannot fold it."[5]

It is the Milky Way. "Learn . . . learn," Rudolfo's mother urged him. "Be as wise as your grandfather."[6]

Though it was a shock to encounter English when he started school, Rudolfo quickly learned the language and fulfilled his mother's expectations. He excelled at his studies. After school and in the summer, he roamed the bush, hunting, fishing, playing, and sometimes fighting with the town boys.

In 1952, when Rudolfo was fourteen, the Anaya family left the village and moved to the city of Albuquerque. Martín Anaya could no longer find work on the plains and became a laborer, "a broken man," his son says.[7] The Anayas' oldest son, Larry, already lived in the Barelas neighborhood, where they settled. Larry was well-known and respected in the *barrio*, the quarter, so the street gangs left Rudolfo alone.

At Washington Junior High, then at Albuquerque High School, Rudolfo played sports, cruised with his friends in their cars, and danced to rock and roll, which was then brand new. When his friends found out that he could "turn a phrase," Anaya says, they hired him to compose love notes to their girlfriends. But the girls weren't dumb. They "knew very well who was writing the sweet words, and many a heart I was supposed to capture fell in love with me."[8]

Early one summer in high school, Rudolfo and his friends went to swim in a nearby irrigation ditch. Rudolfo dove in first, and in an instant, "the world disappeared," he remembers.[9] The water was not as deep as he had believed, and he fractured two vertebrae in his neck when he hit bottom. He was temporarily paralyzed and spent the summer first encased in a full-body cast, then in rehabilitation. When he returned home months later, he walked with a cane at first, but at least he walked.

Anaya graduated from high school in 1956. He attended business school for two years with the intention of becoming an accountant. But he wanted more from his education. He switched to the University of New Mexico and worked at a variety of jobs as he attended college part-time.

Anaya's freshman English course opened a new world of literature to him. He banded together with other Chicano students, Americans of Mexican descent, who were interested in writing. In the 1950s, the university "tolerated rather than accepted" them, Anaya believes.[10] Chicano students were even criticized for retaining the hint of an accent. Anaya wrote poetry and several novels in college, all of which he later burned when he decided they weren't good enough.

After graduation in 1963 with a bachelor's degree in English, Anaya became a public school teacher. He married Patricia Lawless, a guidance counselor, in 1966. He studied part-time for a master's degree in English, which he received from the University of New Mexico in 1968.

All this time, Anaya labored on the novel that would become his masterpiece. He set his story of a Chicano boy growing up, on the *llanos* of his childhood. "I wanted to take those people I had known and make them breathe again," he says. But he was working "in a vacuum."[11] There was no Chicano literature in English at all in the early 1960s from which to draw inspiration. How would he find the voice to make that unique culture come to life?

Late one night, Anaya was struggling with his writing. Suddenly, he heard a noise. He turned and saw an old woman enter. She was dressed in black and smelled of sweet herbs. She was a *curandera*, a traditional healer, and her name was Ultima. She put her hand on Anaya's shoulder and he "felt the power of the whirlwind," he says. Was Ultima a heavenly visitor, a vision, or a hallucination? Whatever she was, from that day on, Anaya feels, he wrote from the collective memory of his people. He had gone into a trance, he now believes, that had unlocked his creativity.[12]

Anaya wrote and rewrote *Bless Me, Ultima* for seven years. He received enough publishers' rejection letters to "wallpaper the proverbial room," he remembers.[13] Many editors objected to the abundant use of Spanish words, which was unheard-of in an English-language novel at that time. Finally, Anaya submitted his novel to a small Chicano press. Not only did they publish it in 1972, but he won the recently created *Premio Quinto Sol* for it. This award

Award Winning

Best Seller 175,000 sold!!

BLESS ME, ULTIMA

Rudolfo A. Anaya

A PUBLICATION OF TONATIUH INTERNATIONAL

Anaya's novel, *Bless Me, Ultima* won the *Premio Quinto Sol* (as this book jacket shows). The *Premio Quinto Sol* is an award that honors the finest Chicano writing of the year.

honors the finest Chicano writing of the year. *Bless Me, Ultima* went on to become an underground classic, selling more than a million copies over the years. Anaya is now generally regarded as "one of the founding fathers of Chicano literature."[14]

Professionally, Anaya switched from teaching to being a guidance counselor. He earned a second master's degree in counseling in 1972. Then, in 1974, he became a professor of English at the University of New Mexico.

Anaya's next two novels incorporated his interest in myth. *Heart of Atzlán* (1976) told the story of a rural Chicano family moving to Albuquerque in the 1950s. Atzlán is the mythical homeland of the Aztecs, whose stories told of their migration from the north, perhaps New Mexico. *Tortuga* (1979) is the Spanish word for "turtle." It is the name given to its teenage hero because of the full-body cast that forms his shell after a diving accident. With *Bless Me, Ultima*, these three novels form what Anaya considers an autobiographical trilogy.

"I think of myself as a novelist," Anaya says, "but from the beginning I wanted to try many things."[15] During the 1980s, he wrote plays, screenplays, children's stories, and anthologized the writings of other Chicanos and New Mexicans. He also lectured at different universities and traveled with his wife in Europe and China.

Anaya resumed novel writing with *Alburquerque*, published in 1992. This story about a young boxer who seeks his true family heritage after finding out he is adopted, used the original spelling of the city's name. Anaya retired from university teaching in 1993 to write full-time. After many years of literary success, he finally won his first contract with a major publisher, Warner Books. They have brought out his trio of politically and environmentally themed mysteries featuring the Chicano detective Sonny Baca: *Zia Summer* in 1995, *Rio Grande Fall* in 1996, and *Shaman Winter* in 1999.

Anaya and his wife, whom he credits as his first and best editor, live in an adobe house they designed themselves. It sits atop a high mesa west of Albuquerque. From there, Anaya has a stunning vista of his beloved home state. He can see the city, the Rio Grande with cottonwood forests lining its banks, and the Sandia Mountains to the east.

Writing is "the best life that the fates (*el destino*) could have granted [me]," Anaya believes.[16] He hopes that his work inspires Chicano young people, especially aspiring writers. He notes that in his novels, many of his protagonists have mentors or spiritual guides. He would like to be such a guide himself. "In a sense," he says, "[that is] the role of the writer."[17]

Sandra Cisneros

3

Sandra Cisneros
(December 20, 1954–   )

Some of the finest young writers in the country, including Sandra Cisneros, faced each other in a classroom at the University of Iowa. The students hotly debated the idea that imagination was like a house. Several compared imagination to the houses they had grown up in, with secret, special places like attics and cellars, nooks and crannies. Cisneros wondered what that would be like.[1]

She thought back to her family's cramped Chicago apartments. She remembered the first house they owned, tiny and run-down, her bedroom the size of a closet. There had been nothing special about it. How could she ever be a writer like these other students? They were "hothouse flowers," she remembers. "I was a yellow weed among the city's cracks."[2]

At that moment she realized that although she was different, she could use this difference to her advantage as a writer. It was there that "my writing acquired a voice," she says.[3]

Sandra Cisneros was born in Chicago on December 20, 1954. Her father, Alfredo Cisneros del Moral, fled Mexico as a university student. He had wasted a year of college by gambling and carousing, and feared the wrath of his father, a stern army officer. Alfredo Cisneros avoided deportation from the United States by serving in the U.S. army during World War II. After the war he passed through Chicago where he met Elvira Cordero Anguiano, a Mexican American, at a dance. They married and Alfredo became an upholsterer.

The couple had six sons and a daughter, Sandra. Her only sister, born a year and a half after her, died as a baby. The six boys, two older and four younger, paired off as close companions, "leaving me odd woman out—forever," she remembers.[4]

Her family's wandering lifestyle increased her isolation. Alfredo Cisneros missed his homeland and his mother. Periodically, his longing became so great that he would pull his children out of school to visit Mexico for weeks at a time. The constant uprooting prevented Sandra from making friends or excelling in school. "I retreated inside myself," she says.[5] Yet "my parents . . . taught us to believe in ourselves," she remembers, "Even when the education system did not."[6]

Sandra Cisneros was born in Chicago, Illinois.

Sandra grew up completely bilingual. She and her brothers spoke Spanish to their father, English to their mother; Spanish visiting Mexico, English at school in Chicago. "[I have] twice as many words to pick from [and] two ways of looking at the world," she says.[7]

Sandra attended Josephium High School, a Catholic girls' school in Chicago. While there, her tenth-grade teacher praised the poetry she had begun writing. Sandra contributed to the school literary magazine and eventually became its editor. She graduated in 1972 and went to Loyola University.

Cisneros lived at home and commuted to the Chicago college. She was one of only a few students of color there. As a junior, Cisneros enrolled in a creative writing class. Her professor suggested she apply to the University of Iowa's Master of Fine Arts program in writing. Without realizing how competitive or prestigious the program was, she applied. When Cisneros received her bachelor's degree in 1976, she left home alone for the first time, headed for the University of Iowa.

Cisneros spent her first year there "hobbling around disguised as everybody else," imitating the other students and teachers, she says.[8] Then came the breakthrough she experienced when her classmates were debating imagination. Her writer's voice freed, she blossomed creatively. Cisneros began writing the stories and poems that became her first two books "that same night," she remembers. They burst out of her "like a deluge."[9]

She received her master's degree in 1978. Many of her classmates sought positions teaching creative writing in universities, but Cisneros held back. She feared she wasn't "good enough."[10] Instead, she took a job as a high school teacher and counselor in Chicago. Later, she worked as a recruiter of minority students for Loyola University. Then, a creative writing grant enabled her to travel and live in Europe from 1982 to 1983.

All the while, she honed and shaped the stories that were to form *The House on Mango Street*, published in 1984. This set of interconnected vignettes tells the story of Esperanza, a young woman coming of age in the Chicago barrio. Like Cisneros, she sought "a home in the heart," where her creativity would be nurtured.[11] Cisneros wanted readers to be able to approach the stories either separately or together. "You would understand each story like a little pearl, or you could look at the whole thing like a necklace," she explains.[12] *The House on Mango Street* quickly became a favorite of college and high school teachers, who used it in their classes.

Still, Cisneros was unable to support herself as a writer. First, she took a job as literature director of an arts center in San Antonio, Texas. After a year, she won a fellowship and moved to Mexico to write poetry. She then took a series of appointments as a visiting university professor, but she found that teaching drained her for creative writing. She also disliked the classroom's rigid schedule. Her first full volume of poetry was published in 1987. *My Wicked, Wicked Ways* won good reviews and featured a cover photo of Cisneros saucily posed in cowboy boots with wine-reddened lips. But again, the book failed to earn enough for her to live.

Cisneros fell into a depression, fearing she would never be able to write for a living. She still lacked "self-esteem," she wrote. Her writing seemed "useless in trying to feed and clothe me [or] get adult things like health insurance."[13] Winning another grant at the end of 1987 shook her out of her despondence.

Cisneros contacted a New York agent who quickly sold a selection of Cisneros's recent stories to Random House. When the stories were published in 1991 as *Woman Hollering Creek*, it marked the first time a major New York publisher had brought out the work of a Mexican-American woman writer. Small presses had issued Cisneros's first two books. *Woman Hollering Creek* won rave reviews and became a best-seller. Random House also issued Cisneros's next poetry collection, *Loose Woman*, in 1994.

Cisneros moved back to San Antonio. During her summers off as a visiting professor, she had always returned there, liking its vibrant Chicano culture and low cost of living. She bought a historic Victorian house in the city's picturesque King William district. Finally, winning a John and Catherine MacArthur Foundation fellowship in 1995, for a whopping $255,000, gave her financial security.

Despite several serious romantic relationships, Cisneros has often boasted that she's "nobody's wife and nobody's mother."[14] She admits that "growing up Mexican and feminist is almost a contradiction in terms," and is saddened that her life choices have sometimes seemed to alienate her from the culture she loves.[15] Yet, she says, "It's so wonderful now . . . that living against the grain has taken me exactly where I wanted to go."[16]

Cisneros looks back on the difficult road she traveled and continues to travel as a writer. "Writing is hard work," she says, "And a woman's life is not romantic . . . Every day I am both defeated and victorious. I invent as I go along."[17]

Through the 1990s, Cisneros has grappled with a historical novel based on the lives of her parents. She longs to tell all the "stories that don't get told," she says.[18] As she writes about Mexican Americans though, she hopes to speak to all Americans, indeed all citizens of the world. "For those of us living between worlds, our job in the universe is to help others see with more than their eyes . . . to help others become visionary."[19]

Judith Ortiz Cofer

Judith Ortiz Cofer
(February 24, 1952–)

Young Judith Ortiz crept through the dilapidated neighborhood between her apartment and the library. Somewhere, in one of those run-down little houses, lived Lorraine, the girl who was waiting to beat Judith up. Their teacher had chosen Judith to tutor the slower Lorraine in spelling. Lorraine's revenge for this humiliation was to threaten her tutor with a whipping. It was Saturday morning and Judith's strict mother allowed her one hour to visit the public library. If she took more than fifteen minutes travel time, her brother would be sent to find her and march her home.

Judith was terrified of Lorraine, but her need for books overcame her fear. She snuck past the rusty abandoned cars and discarded refrigerators until she saw the library building. Guarded by two stone lions, it rose "like a mirage among the ruins of the city," she remembers.[1] Clutching her children's card, Judith slipped safely inside. Now, she felt secure among the "inexhaustible treasure of books."[2]

Judith Ortiz Cofer was born in Hormigueros, Puerto Rico, on the island's southwest coast, on February 24, 1952. Her father, Jesus Ortiz, was serving with the United States Army and never saw her until she was two years old. When his tour of duty ended, he returned to school in Puerto Rico. Judith's mother, Fanny, became pregnant again and after the birth of his son, Mr. Ortiz quit school. He reenlisted, this time in the United States Navy. Forced to give up his dream of education to support his family, he transferred his dreams to his children.

For the next twelve years, Judith, her mother, and her brother alternated between living in Hormigueros and in Paterson, New Jersey, depending upon where Mr. Ortiz was stationed by the navy. When he worked at the Brooklyn Navy Yard in New York, the family lived in Paterson. When his ship was at sea, they returned to Hormigueros.

The Ortiz family spoke Spanish in Puerto Rico and inside the home, wherever they lived. But the children always spoke English in school, since even on the island they attended an English-language school. "My father felt that our anchor in life was an education," Cofer remembers.[3] In spite of the continual, abrupt changes of school, he expected his children to excel.

Mr. Ortiz spoke fluent English and insisted that Judith and her brother do the same. Mrs. Ortiz, however, refused to learn the language. From an early age, Judith was compelled to translate for her mother when her father was away. "It was hard being a bilingual child," she says, "but it opened my mind to two different [points of view.]"[4]

In Hormigueros, the family lived with Mrs. Ortiz's parents in a rambling blue house on a hillside surrounded by coffee fields. Judith's grandfather was a builder, who often wrote poetry and songs for special occasions. Her grandmother, though she could barely read or write, was a spellbinding storyteller. If she had a story, Cofer says, she would "embellish it, change it, try it out on us, change it again, transform it."[5]

Every day in late afternoon, their chores done, the women of the family settled in their rocking chairs. Sipping *café con leche*, milky Puerto Rican coffee, they told stories. The young girls were shooed out of the room but were fully expected to eavesdrop. The women intended their stories to teach their daughters a woman's role in life. Whenever the girls heard their grandmother's voice begin, "Well, let me tell you what really happened . . . ," they were "hooked," Cofer says. From her grandmother, she learned the power of the story. Once you have your

Judith Ortiz grew up moving back and forth between Hormigueros, Puerto Rico, and Paterson, New Jersey. As a teenager, she moved to Augusta, Georgia, where she graduated from high school.

audience under that "ancient spell," Cofer believes, "they're yours."[6]

In Paterson, the Ortiz family lived in a small apartment above a deli. Mr. Ortiz stayed at the navy yard during the week, returning to Paterson on weekends. When he was gone, the apartment became a replica of Mrs. Ortiz's island house, her *casa.* Spanish-language records played, Spanish-language romance novels, magazines, and newspapers were read, candles burned before holy pictures.

Mr. Ortiz retired from the navy in 1968, when Judith was fourteen. Rather than return to Puerto Rico, however, the family moved to Augusta, Georgia, where Mr. Ortiz had relatives. He was anxious that his children continue their American education and felt it was a safer place for teenagers than the city. To Judith, it was like "moving from one planet to another."[7] She found, though, that Georgians were less likely to have negative preconceptions about Hispanics. Instead, they were often intrigued by her background.

Judith graduated from Augusta's Butler High School in 1970. She won a scholarship to nearby Augusta College. During her sophomore year, she married Charles Cofer but continued to attend college full-time. Their daughter, Tanya, was born in 1974, shortly before Judith's graduation with a degree in English. The Cofer family then moved to Fort Lauderdale, Florida.

In 1976, Jesus Ortiz was killed in an automobile accident. Mrs. Ortiz returned to Hormigueros and settled near her family. Cofer marvels that her mother soon went "totally native," shedding any trace of twenty-some years residence on the mainland.[8]

Cofer received a master's degree in English in 1977 from Florida Atlantic University. She began teaching part-time at a local community college. It was then, she says, that "I kept looking for what was missing in my life and discovered it was writing."[9] She began to rise very early, before her family awoke, to write poetry.

Cofer became close friends with Betty Owen, her English department head, and they often lunched together and talked. Cofer frequently shared stories of her bicultural childhood. Owen suggested that Cofer try writing about her experiences. When Cofer admitted that she already had, Owen offered to read what she had written. After much persuasion, Cofer agreed. She describes herself as "astonished" when Owen declared that with a little revision, her poems would merit publication.[10]

Cofer submitted a poem, "Latin Women Pray," to the *New Mexico Humanities Review*. They accepted and published it in 1978. For the next several years, many of her poems appeared in literary journals. She also published four poetry pamphlets, or chapbooks, with small presses.

The Cofer family moved back to Georgia in 1984 when Charles Cofer inherited his family's farm in rural Louisville. "It's a beautiful, beautiful place," Judith says.[11] It also makes her feel closer to her grandmother, a farmer's daughter. Cofer began teaching at the University of Georgia in Athens.

Cofer published her first full-length poetry collections, *Terms of Survival* and *Reaching for the Mainland*, in 1987. Soon she began experimenting with writing a novel while continuing her poetry. She believes poetry taught her discipline as a writer. Yet her poems most often tell stories. Like her grandmother, she is a "compulsive storyteller."[12]

Her novel *The Line of the Sun* was published in 1989. Its heroine is a Puerto Rican girl in Paterson, New Jersey, whose ne'er-do-well uncle is a profound influence on her life. Cofer's proud mother told her, "Everyone here [on the island] is amazed that you write as if you've been here all your life."[13] Cofer admits that though she visits yearly, it is more through memory and imagination that she maintains her connection.

Cofer began receiving invitations to read her poems at literary gatherings. When she did, she often prefaced each poem with the childhood story that had inspired it. Novelist Hilma Wolitzer heard her read and suggested she write a memoir mixed with poetry. That way, both genres would illuminate her experiences in contrasting ways. Cofer took the suggestion. *Silent Dancing: A Partial Remembrance of a Puerto Rican Childhood* was published in 1990.

Selections from *Silent Dancing* and Cofer's other writings began to be published in textbooks and collections for students. A children's book editor approached her to ask if she'd like to try writing for young people. After *An Island Like You: Stories of the Barrio* was published in 1995, this collection of tales of Puerto Rican teens won the Pura Belpre Award for distinguished writing by a Hispanic author.

"You can and must find a channel that takes you back and forth between cultures," says Cofer of her biculturalism.[14] Yet she hopes her writing "transcend[s] labels." She imagines a Puerto Rican reader being reminded of his or her grandmother by one of her poems or stories. Then she imagines one of her daughter's friends "from Alabama or Arizona" seeing her own grandmother in the same piece. Cofer wants her work to speak to all readers, to be "something [any] people can read and get something out of."[15]

5

Oscar Hijuelos

(August 24, 1951–)

Four-year-old Oscar Hijuelos lay near death. He had contracted nephritis, a severe kidney disease, during a family visit to relatives in Cuba. His desperate parents agreed to send him from their New York City home to a Catholic children's hospital in Connecticut.

Gradually, he recovered. He stayed in the hospital and a nearby convalescent home for a year and a half. During that time, his family could only see him from a distance. When he returned home, he had forgotten how to speak Spanish, his native tongue. When his parents spoke to him in Spanish, he still understood them, though. Together they worked out a way to communicate. His parents would talk to him in Spanish and Oscar would answer in English.

Oscar Hijuelos

"They were so happy that I was around," Hijuelos remembers, that they accepted the compromise.[1]

Oscar Hijuelos was born in New York on August 24, 1951. His parents both came from Cuba's Oriente province. They had immigrated to the United States in 1943. Pascual Hijuelos had taken an inheritance with him and hoped to start a business. He soon squandered his money, however, by making bad investments and giving gifts to fellow Cubans. He went to work as a cook at the Biltmore Hotel in New York City, a job he held until his death.

When Oscar returned from the hospital, his mother, Magdalena, remained very protective. She kept him home for all but a few weeks of first grade and taught him herself. She read comics aloud to him, so both of them could learn to read English at the same time. She also encouraged him to draw. He was a solitary child. His only friend used to come to his window to play. Together they set up model soldiers, one boy inside, one outside.

Magdalena Hijuelos wrote her own poetry and often recited it to Oscar and his older brother, Joseph. She frequently told them stories of her Cuban girlhood. Although he always liked to read growing up, Oscar never considered becoming a writer. He thought, instead, that he might become a cartoonist. He drew and collected comic books, which his father often brought him as gifts.

The family did not get a television set until Oscar was in school. Once they did, one of their favorite shows was *I Love Lucy*, starring Lucille Ball and her Cuban-born husband, Desi Arnaz. "I thought that Desi was the star!" Hijuelos says.[2]

The family lived in an apartment in Morningside Heights, a multiethnic Manhattan neighborhood between Columbia University and Harlem. As he grew up, Oscar demanded and got more freedom. Oscar had, he says, a "typical troubled-wonderful-dangerous New York childhood."[3] He attended Catholic grade school, then public junior high and high school. He remembers boxing lessons in a nearby church basement, playing in a Harlem softball league, and going to Times Square to see the ball drop on New Year's Eve.

Oscar learned to play the guitar and piano. He belonged to a series of bands, mostly with Puerto Rican friends, who played pop hits as well as Latin music. His friends called him "El Cubano," despite his reddish hair and fair skin. His untypically Cuban coloring sometimes made him feel "like a spy" in the city, he says. Riding the bus, he would hear Irish kids in front of him ridicule "spicks," then Latinos from other neighborhoods would chase him and call him "Whitey."[4] He was also puzzled and angered by his parents' immigrant fearfulness toward life in New York, and their "unending sense of second classness," he remembers.[5]

Pascual Hijuelos died when Oscar was eighteen. Though his father had been an alcoholic for many years, Oscar always felt that there was "a lot of affection in my household and that makes a big difference." His father also never missed a day of work and his son inherited that work ethic.[6]

Both his parents had graduated from high school in Cuba and his father had always urged him to aim for college. But his father's death threw Hijuelos off track. For several years, he "blindly stumbled around," he says. He dropped in and out of Bronx Community College, working odd jobs and playing in bands. Finally, he settled on studying English at

Oscar Hijuelos grew up in Morningside Heights, a multiethnic Manhattan neighborhood.

City College of New York, where a writing course came as a revelation to him. Haunted for years by feelings of "anger, shame and inadequacy," he now saw the glimmer of a way to deal with them. "I stumbled on a way of understanding [my life] through the written word," he says.[7]

Hijuelos graduated from City College in 1975 and went on to its renowned Master of Arts program in writing. He threw himself into his work and quickly accumulated four shopping bags worth of manuscripts. In 1975 he also married an actress he had dated in college, but the marriage ended in divorce in less than a year.

One day Hijuelos wandered into the magnificent Cathedral of Saint John the Divine, near his home. Sitting there in the world's largest gothic church, he pulled a palm-reader's flyer from his pocket. On the back of it, he wrote the first words of an autobiographical novel. One of his classmates heard him read from an early draft of the book. She and her husband had founded their own small press and offered to publish the novel.

Our House in the Last World, the story of a Cuban immigrant family, was published to universal praise in 1983. By this time, Hijuelos had finished graduate school and had gone to work for an advertising agency. The agency's specialty was putting posters in New York buses and subways. They cut Hijuelos a deal. He exchanged his services for free advertising for his book.

The critical success of his first novel also won Hijuelos two large and prestigious grants. Then a major publisher gave him a contract for his next book. He now had enough money to quit his day job and has been writing full-time ever since. One of the awards allowed him to live in Italy for a year. Away from his Cuban and New York roots for the first time, Hijuelos began the book that would make him famous, *The Mambo Kings Play Songs of Love.*

This novel of two Cuban musician brothers, Cesar and Nestor Castillo, who move to New York to seek their fortunes during the mambo craze of the 1950s, became a best-seller in 1989. Early the next year, Hijuelos took a phone call from the chairman of his new publishing house. "You did it, kid! You won the big one—the Pulitzer!" the chairman said.[8] Hijuelos became the first and only Hispanic American to win the Pulitzer Prize for fiction. The novel has been translated into over ten languages.

One of the highlights of *The Mambo Kings* is a hilarious scene in which the fictional brothers appear on the *I Love Lucy* show, playing with Desi Arnaz's character, Ricky Ricardo, in his nightclub. Hijuelos has received letters from readers insisting that they have actually seen this episode, but he states, "I made that up."[9] He was also pleased that both Desi Arnaz and Lucille Ball read the novel before their deaths and liked it.

The movie rights to *The Mambo Kings* sold for a quarter million dollars. The film, released in 1992, starred Antonio Banderas. Hijuelos was involved in the production and played a cameo role in the film, but was not 100 percent satisfied with the result. "I give it three stars," he says.[10]

Hijuelos published three more novels in the 1990s: *The Fourteen Sisters of Emilio Montez O'Brien* (1993); *Mr. Ives' Christmas* (1995); and *The Empress of the Splendid Season* (1999).

Hijuelos considers his lifelong New York residence to be as influential in his writing as his Cuban heritage. He dislikes being expected by some people to confine himself to "certain cultural limitations" because of his Hispanic background.[11] Yet he is pleased that fellow Latino writers take pride in his success.[12] He has promoted the careers of young Latino authors, such as novelist Elena Castedo. He also refuses to take a stand on Cuban-American relations. "I can see both sides," he says.[13]

Music remains a big part of Hijuelos's life. He still plays the guitar and keyboards and often writes songs. He and a friend composed the Academy Award-nominated "Beautiful Maria of My Soul," that is the fictional Mambo Kings' hit record in the book and movie. The multitalented Hijuelos also still draws and cartoons.

Hijuelos married Lori Carlson in 1998. She is an editor, translator, and author of books for young people. They still live on Manhattan's Upper West Side, not far from where Hijuelos grew up.

Even so, "there is a part of me that has traveled far from my roots," he admits. Hijuelos has hobnobbed with movie stars and dined at the White House more than once. At one presidential reception, he met his idol, the Colombian Nobel Prize winner Gabriel García Márquez. "So I am standing there talking to this great writer," he remembered, "[but] there is always a part of me wondering how I got to this moment."[14]

Nicholasa Mohr

Nicholasa Mohr
(November 1, 1938–   )

Young Nicholasa waited for her mother to call her. Her mother was near death and had asked to speak privately to each member of the family. Nicholasa's father and stepfather were already dead. If her mother died too, she would be an orphan at fourteen. Only days before, Doña Nicolasa, as the family called her mother in the Puerto Rican tradition, had come home from the hospital where she was being treated for cancer. She had seemed to rally. She had asked Nicholasa, her only daughter, to brush and braid her long black hair for her. Then she went into seclusion. For two days she met with each of her children. Finally, it was young Nicholasa's turn. She had been called last.

Doña Nicolasa wept to think that she would leave her daughter alone and unprotected. But, dying, she handed Nicholasa a precious charge, a vision. Nicholasa, who loved to draw, should imagine herself an artist, a success, she said. Next, she should imagine a life with her dream unfulfilled. Her daughter had a creative gift, Doña Nicolasa believed. "Never forget what you want, never," she urged Nicholasa.[1]

The next day Doña Nicolasa slipped into a coma. A week later she died. But her mother's last words gave her "a rich legacy," Nicholasa Mohr says. "With this inheritance, I have always found the strength to . . . follow my own star."[2]

Nicholasa Rivera Golpe, named for her mother, was born in New York City's Spanish Harlem on November 1, 1938. A careless clerk had misspelled her name on the birth certificate, but she chose to keep the different, more American, spelling.

Her mother had fled an abusive husband in Puerto Rico. Working in a New York garment factory, Doña Nicolasa met Pedro Golpe, an immigrant from Spain. They married and Golpe sent for his wife's four sons, who had been left behind in Puerto Rico. The Golpes had two more boys. To Doña Nicolasa's great joy, she then gave birth to a girl.[3]

The couple's marriage, however, became troubled and they separated several times while Nicholasa was young. Don Pedro suspected his wife of unfaithfulness. He believed that Nicholasa's biological father was a Puerto Rican family friend, whom she refers to in her autobiography as "Martin."

Though her mother vehemently denied it, Mohr now believes it was probably true.[4] Nicholasa had almond-shaped eyes like Martin's. More than anyone else, even her beloved mother, Martin gave her unconditional love. He called her princess, gave her presents, let her win every card game and admired her singing, dancing and drawing. "In Martin's eyes . . .I was beautiful and I was smart," Mohr remembers.[5] But he suddenly vanished from her life when she was six. His disappearance was the price paid for peace in the family.

Nicholasa, her six brothers, her mother and stepfather, her aunt and cousin, and various boarders or relatives in need of help lived together, crowded into a series of narrow tenement apartments. With such a large family, her mother had little time left for Nicholasa. To keep her daughter busy, she often gave her pencils, crayons, and paper and urged her to copy pictures from the comics. Young as she was, Nicholasa drew exceptionally well and knew she always had a way to win her mother's attention and praise. And with drawing "I could create my own world [that] permitted me . . . space, freedom and adventure," she says.[6]

Soon, Nicholasa noticed the funny shapes written inside the "balloons" coming from the mouths of the comic-strip characters. Her brother Vincent explained they were words. He began to teach her letters. The adults in the family spoke Spanish to one another and to the children, but Nicholasa's brothers often spoke English to one another. By the time she started school, Nicholasa could read English and speak both languages.

About this time the family moved from Manhattan to the Bronx. Mohr remembers public school as a place of boredom and petty rules. She recalls being humiliated before her class for counting higher than the teacher instructed and being punished for speaking Spanish to a new classmate who knew no English. Teachers openly expressed prejudice against Hispanic students. Once, she overheard a hostile teacher say of her drawing, "Nicholasa has talent, so she can't be all bad."[7]

Nicholasa's stepfather died of heart disease when she was eight. Her mother worked as a seamstress to support the family. From time to time, ill health forced her to accept public assistance.

Two years after her husband died, Doña Nicolasa took a dying Martin back into the family. By this time, however, he had become a bad-tempered alcoholic. Though he and Nicholasa did not regain their closeness, she mourned his death. He was buried with a picture she drew of him as the happy, loving man she remembered.

Doña Nicolasa became ill herself when Nicholasa was in ninth grade. Her married sons, Vincent and Gilbert, moved back home with their wives to help support and nurse her. A despondent Nicholasa found it difficult to study and her excellent grades began to slip.

Nevertheless, she still hoped to attend the prestigious High School of Music and Art. It was a shock, then, when her school counselor refused to recommend her. Mohr remembers the counselor telling her it was "for my own good."[8] Puerto Rican women sew beautifully, the counselor declared. Nicholasa should attend a vocational high school to learn the fashion trade. Without a parent to fight for her, Nicholasa had to accept the counselor's decision. She attended graduation wearing a white satin dress with matching purse and headband that her gravely ill mother had struggled to sew herself. Doña Nicolasa died without knowing of her daughter's disappointment.

After her mother's death, Nicholasa went to live with an aunt and uncle who cared little for her. At vocational high school, she managed to avoid studying clothing construction by taking fashion illustration instead. "To this day I hate. . . sewing," she says.[9] She found her art classes unchallenging and was relieved when she graduated in 1956.

She kept her dream alive, though. While working as a waitress and in factories, she attended New York's Art Students' League. She saved money and was able to study at the Taller de Grafica in Mexico City. When she returned in 1958, she resumed art study at New York's New School for Social Research. There she met a doctoral student in clinical child psychology, Irwin Mohr, a native Brooklynite. They fell in love and married after a short courtship. Their two sons, David and Jason, were born in Brooklyn.

Nicholasa Mohr continued to study and produce art while raising her children. She worked in printmaking, oil paint, and watercolor. Often she used a collage technique, a composition made of different materials, that included text. She became quite successful and her works were exhibited and sold in art galleries. In 1970 the Mohr family moved to Teaneck, New Jersey, where she remodeled a studio in their large new house.

A prominent publisher who collected her prints and paintings sent Mohr a message through her agent. He was intrigued by the words in her artwork. Had she ever thought of writing about her life? Mohr

realized that virtually no literature had yet been published in English about Puerto Rican women or children. She sent him a sample of stories about her childhood, but the publisher rejected them. He had hoped for tales of sex,

Nicholasa Golpe graduated from junior high school wearing the white satin dress her dying mother sewed for her. Her mother urged her to follow her dreams.

drugs, and gangs that he could turn into a lurid best-seller. An insulted Mohr put the manuscript away.[10] Only a week later, though, a children's publisher asked her to design a book jacket. Mohr brought her manuscript to the interview and was quickly offered a contract to write her first novel.

Nilda, published in 1973, told the story of a Puerto Rican girl in New York City during World War II. Mohr says that it is "almost real," but not quite autobiographical. Like the young Nicholasa, Nilda is a talented artist. Mohr says she gave her heroine "creative force because that was what made me not only survive, but also helped me thrive."[11] The novel won high praise and has been in print for almost thirty years.

Mohr drew the book jacket and illustrations for *Nilda* and also for her next book, *El Bronx Remembered* (1975). Then she decided to give up her artwork and dismantled her studio. "I had become an avid storyteller," she realized. "Painting with words instead of images had become my new [medium]."[12] She also preferred the larger audience that writing attracted. Thousands of readers could own her work now, instead of just a few wealthy collectors.

Irwin Mohr died in 1978. Since her sons by then were nearly grown, Nicholasa Mohr moved back to the city. "My heart is in Nueva York," she admits. She loves its "immense diversity [and] richness."[13]

She bought a brownstone townhouse in Brooklyn's Park Slope section in 1980.

"Work—it's my most faithful companion," she says.[14] Her writing has been immensely varied in the past twenty years. She has written novels for the middle grades like *Felita* and its sequel, *Going Home*, as well as a chapter book for the early grades, *The Magic Shell*. She has also written biography, autobiography, traditional and original folktales, and had plays and screenplays produced. Her first book for adults, *Rituals of Survival*, a short-story collection, was published in 1985. In addition to writing, she often serves as a visiting faculty member at universities from California to London.

"The easiest part of my work is wanting so much to do it and loving to do it," she says. "It's wonderful. It's magic. It's the magical element of creativity that has been the most joyful experience I have had in my life."[15]

Richard Rodriguez
(July 31, 1944–)

It was a Saturday morning in 1951 when three nuns knocked on the door of the Rodriguez home in Sacramento, California. Mr. and Mrs. Rodriguez, devout Catholics, ushered the visitors into the living room and seated them on the sofa. The sisters had come to express concern over the slow progress the Rodriguez children were making in parochial school. "Richard especially seems so timid and shy," said one.[1]

The nuns asked if the Rodriguez family spoke only Spanish at home. They did, the parents admitted. The nuns then gently suggested that perhaps if the family spoke more English, the children would do better in school. Believing the request to be the wish of their church, Mr. and Mrs. Rodriguez

Richard Rodriguez

agreed. In fact, they went a step further. As soon as the sisters left, they announced to their children that the family would speak only English together in the future.

"In an instant," Richard Rodriguez wrote, "they agreed to give up the language . . . that had revealed and accentuated our family's closeness."[2] Because the Rodriguez parents' basic English could express far less precision and detail than their fluent Spanish, their son believes that the change ended true communication between parent and child. But it paid off academically. The four children became good students. Richard Rodriguez now feels that their parents' sacrifice was not only justified, it was necessary. "To succeed in the classroom," he wrote, "I needed psychologically to sever my ties with Spanish."[3]

Richard Rodriguez was born Ricardo Rodriguez on July 31, 1944, in San Francisco. He later kept the English version of his first name, after the nuns used it in school. His parents, Leopoldo and Victoria Moran Rodriguez, both left Mexico for the United States as teenagers. Mrs. Rodriguez graduated from high school in California and took secretarial courses at night. She worked as a typist before her marriage. Mr. Rodriguez worked various manufacturing and warehouse jobs.

The family moved to Sacramento when Richard was a preschooler. Mr. Rodriguez started his own business making false teeth. The family prospered and bought a modest house near a wealthy section of the city. They were the only Hispanic household in the neighborhood. Richard remembers their home life, with his older brother and sister and younger sister, as exceptionally happy and close.

Richard was in first grade when the switch to English at home changed his life. Rodriguez has nothing but praise for his parochial school education. His Irish-born teachers, the Sisters of Mercy, taught him "the Queen's English," he says.[4] He became a top student and a voracious reader. He decided to read only "important books," though and so missed out on childhood classics like *Alice in Wonderland* till he was in college.[5] At Christian Brothers High School in Sacramento, he continued to excel.

In 1963 he went to college at Stanford University in Palo Alto, California. Again, he succeeded. Popular and at ease in the university environment, he was elected student-body president. During his first years at Stanford, he was one of only a few minority students. The brown-skinned Rodriguez was sometimes asked if he was from India.

In the mid-1960s, while he attended college, the Chicano-rights movement was launched. Affirmative-action programs to increase minority enrollment were proposed for colleges. Suddenly, to Rodriguez's discomfort, he had a "group identity." By the time he graduated in 1967, "my presence was annually noted" in an official count of minority students, he says.[6]

Rodriguez decided to become a college professor. When he applied for graduate-school scholarships, they came easily. Admissions interviewers assured him that his becoming a professor would benefit the Chicano community. Rodriguez at first "gratefully believed" them, he says. Doing so relieved the "guilt" he felt at accepting scholarships he wondered if he truly deserved.[7] Did he really have the grades and academic qualifications for admission or did the universities merely want someone to count?

Rodriguez received a master's degree in English from Columbia University in New York City in 1969. Then he went on for his Ph.D. degree to the University of California at Berkeley. After three years of course work, Rodriguez won a prestigious grant to do research in London.

In the quiet of the British Museum, Rodriguez dutifully took notes for his dissertation on Renaissance literature. The silence of the Reading Room bore down on him day after day. Gradually, he began to feel "despair," he says.[8] His writing began to feel "tedious," and weighed down by footnotes. What was the point of writing something so specialized that it would interest no one but a few other scholars? he wondered.[9]

Abruptly, he flew home from London. He lived for a few months with his parents, then decided to return for his final year at Berkeley after all. His experience in London had been disquieting, but he still wanted to teach. Back in graduate school, he began applying for professorships. Job offers from the best universities poured in for him. His fellow graduate students, equally qualified, received few if any.

Again, Rodriguez wrestled with his conscience. Was he benefiting unfairly from affirmative action? There was no reason to apply affirmative action to him, he believed. He was middle class, well educated, English speaking. He was not disadvantaged. Only his parents' country of origin made him different from his colleagues. "I had to protest," he wrote. He determined he would "disqualify myself from the profession as long as affirmative action continued."[10] He quit school for good in 1975.

Rodriguez became a freelance writer. While in graduate school, he had published several magazine articles critiquing affirmative action and bilingual education. Proponents of bilingual education believe that children should be educated in both their native languages and English until their English is fluent. That way, they keep up their skills in other subjects while learning English. Rodriguez rejects this argument. He believes that the family language belongs only in the family. In school, children should learn "public language," which in America is English.[11]

Finally, Rodriguez decided that he would make a definitive statement of his beliefs about race and language. He would write his autobiography and examine how education and language had made him the man he had become. By analyzing his own life, he hoped educators and policy makers would learn something valuable about educating children of a minority group who spoke a foreign language.

Rodriguez moved to San Francisco and took menial jobs, including janitorial work, to support himself while he wrote. For three years, he refined his book. Eight publishers rejected the manuscript. Finally, it was accepted and published in 1982.

The Hunger of Memory: the Education of Richard Rodriguez dropped like a bombshell into the public debate. *The New York Times Book Review* gave it a front-page rave. Across the country, in the *San Francisco Chronicle,* a Chicano professor blasted it with criticism. Some opponents of the book's message attacked Rodriguez personally, calling him a "coconut," brown on the outside, white on the inside.[12] With the book's controversial stand, it was "inevitable" that readers would either love it or hate it, Rodriguez said.[13]

The success of the book and the demand for Rodriguez to give lectures (which paid him well) enabled him to live comfortably from then on. He began to work in television as a producer and commentator, first for the British Broadcasting Corporation (BBC), then for the Public Broadcasting Service (PBS). *Days of Obligation: An Argument with My Mexican Father,* a new collection of his writings, was published in 1992.

Rodriguez was born in San Francisco, California, and returned to live there as an adult.

During the 1990s, Rodriguez worked as an editor with the Pacific News Service. He appears regularly on the PBS program *News Hour With Jim Lehrer*. Because he is seen on television, he has become a celebrity. "I even had a stalker," he jokes grimly. Viewers recognize him and ask, "Aren't you Richard Rodriguez?" He answers, "Sometimes."[14]

Rodriguez still lives in San Francisco and is openly gay. His family knows that a longtime male companion is "part of my life," he says.[15] Although Rodriguez remains a devout Catholic, like his parents, he is disappointed by the Church's stance on homosexuality. "Dare we call homosexuality 'love'?" he asks, and predicts that "the Vatican will one day apologize to homosexuals . . . for centuries of moral cowardice."[16]

Nearly twenty years after the publication of *The Hunger of Memory*, it is still in print and used frequently in college courses. Rodriguez remains steadfast and unapologetic about it. He continues to believe "bilingual education is a bad idea for Hispanic children—that's why it hasn't worked for thirty years. And affirmative action made us lose sight of the true minority, the poor."[17]

Told that college students at one of his lectures had hoisted a sign reading: "Richard Rodriguez is a disgrace to the Chicano community," he responded, "I sort of like that."[18] He continues to go his own way and speak his own mind. "I am this man," he declares, "contrary to what you want to make me."[19]

Esmeralda Santiago

Esmeralda Santiago
(May 17, 1948–   )

Esmeralda Santiago was returning to Puerto Rico for the first time since leaving as a teenager in 1961. Now twenty-eight and an honors graduate of Harvard University, she was eager to make a contribution to her homeland. It was a shock, then, to find that the only job she could get was typing for $3 an hour. "You can have ten Harvard degrees, but you're still a woman in Puerto Rico," her boss said.[1]

Even more shocking was the way strangers instantly pegged her as American, not Puerto Rican. "My Spanish was rusty, my gaze too direct, my personality too assertive," she remembers.[2] Ironically, she found Puerto Rico americanized, too. The way of life she had known as a child had vanished.

These contradictions left her full of questions.

What was Puerto Rican? What was American? And who was she?

Though she was born near San Juan, the Puerto Rican capital, on May 17, 1948, Esmeralda Santiago grew up in rural Macun. The family's home was a corrugated metal cabin on stilts. On sunny days the children could not touch its walls without burning their fingers. The village lacked electricity and running water, so the family used an outhouse and drew water from a public fountain.

Both of Esmeralda's parents had the same surname, Santiago, though they were not related. Pablo, her father, was a construction worker. Her mother, Ramona, nicknamed Monin, was a housewife and a sewing machine operator. The Santiagos were not legally married, but island custom considered them husband and wife by common-law. Esmeralda was the oldest of their seven children. Her family nicknamed her Negi, short for *negrita*, or "little dark one."

Though a loving father, Don Pablo, as he was called, viewed it as his right to do as he pleased and the Santiagos' relationship was stormy. They separated numerous times. Finally, when Negi was thirteen, her mother moved to New York City with her children. "The Puerto Rican *jibara* (country girl) who longed for the green quiet of a tropical afternoon was to become a hybrid who would never forgive the uprooting," she wrote of herself.[3]

Esmeralda Santiago was born near San Juan, Puerto Rico, shown here. Santiago's memoir, *When I Was Puerto Rican*, was one of the first autobiographies of a Puerto Rican woman ever published in English or Spanish. Santiago translates her books herself.

They settled in Brooklyn, with her mother's mother. Negi had been an A student in Puerto Rico, so she was shocked to find that her new public school routinely held foreign students back a grade. With the basic English she had learned at her island school, she persuaded the principal to let her stay in eighth grade. Then she threw herself into mastering both English and how to be an American teenager.

She studied vocabulary from the alphabet books she borrowed from the Brooklyn Public Library. "For leetle seesters," she fibbed to the librarian.[4] She kept a journal to practice her English and record her secret thoughts. She studied the clothes, hair, and walks of her classmates. Most of all, she studied Archie comics. Because Archie and his friends all said "yeah," instead of "yes," Negi taught herself to do the same. "Even now, I really have to make myself say 'yes,'" she admits.[5]

Doña Monin, as her mother was called, found a job sewing in a brassiere factory. When the factory closed, however, she was laid off. Negi had to accompany her to translate at the welfare office, so that public assistance could tide the family over. Doña Monin detested welfare and found a new job as quickly as possible. "When *Mami* worked, things were always better . . . we were happy too," Santiago remembers.[6] Doña Monin also found a new love and gave birth to her eighth child. Sadly, the child's father died shortly after that.

Negi quickly became a top student in Brooklyn, too. Her counselors suggested she apply to one of New York's elite magnet high schools. Which one would it be? One night her family watched the Miss America pageant on television. Dazzled by the glamorous, beautiful contestants, Negi told her counselor she wanted to appear on TV when she grew up. He assumed she wanted to be an actress and advised her to try out for the High School of Performing Arts.[7]

This world-famous school, immortalized in the film and TV series *Fame*, required her to audition with a monologue before its admissions committee. Negi memorized her speech without understanding all of it. At the audition, she was so nervous that she raced through the piece, running the words together. With her heavy accent, it became completely unintelligible. The committee hurried her out of the room and afterward she found out that they had burst out laughing. Yet, admiring her poise and gutsiness, they admitted her.

At the High School of Performing Arts, Negi majored in drama, but she also studied modern dance, which she loved. She excelled as a dancer but had started studying it too late to make it her career.

Nor was she in the school's top rank as an actor. That was because when she arrived at school every day, she was already acting the part of an American teen. "The minute I left the dark, crowded apartment where I lived," she says, "I was in performance, pretending to be someone I wasn't." She was unable to layer one performance over another. "I didn't have the skills to act while acting."[8]

The more American she truly became, the more she resented the rules imposed on her behavior by her strict, tradition-minded mother. " 'Puerto Rican girls don't do that' is like a headline in my brain," she says.[9] Though it would seem to be the opposite of the chaste behavior she insisted on for her daughter, Doña Monin entered another common-law marriage. She would have three more children, for a total of eleven.

Negi graduated from the High School of Performing Arts in 1966 at eighteen. That summer she won a small part in a major feature film, *Up the Down Staircase*, but it was to be her last significant role. For the next three years, she acted and danced sporadically, worked clerical jobs, and took courses at Manhattan Community College. Then, when she was twenty, she fell in love with a Turkish business-man/filmmaker, who was working in the United States. Knowing that her mother would disapprove of the match, she slipped a note of good-bye into the family's mailbox and ran away with him.

For the next five years, Santiago's life was controlled by this emotionally abusive lover. Though he allowed her to work and attend college, he chose her clothes and friends and drove her everywhere himself. Santiago was so in love she thought "that [was] the way the relationship should be," she says.[10] Finally, she decided that the situation was unhealthy and found a way out.

A professor told her that Harvard University in Cambridge, Massachusetts, was recruiting nontradi-tional students and suggested she apply. To her astonishment, they accepted her. In 1974 she started her life over, yet again. Though lonely and fearful, she threw herself into college life, majoring in visual studies.[11] She worked nearly full-time so that she could afford her own apartment, and slept only four hours a night. It was at Harvard that she decided to stop pretending. "I was completely alone," she remembers, and decided to answer for herself the question 'who am I?'"[12]

She made a conscious decision to identify as a Puerto Rican in the future. As a result, Santiago was crushed to be rejected as too American when she moved to the island after graduation in 1976. Nevertheless, she remains defiant. "The people who think I'm not Puerto Rican," she says, "it's their problem, not mine, because I feel Puerto Rican."[13]

Santiago returned to Massachusetts and married her Harvard classmate Frank Cantor in 1978. The couple formed a successful company, Cantomedia, to produce documentary films. They had two children, Lucas and Ila. For twelve years, Santiago lived happily as a suburban working mother. She wrote screenplays for her production company, as well as the occasional newspaper or magazine article.

In 1990 she published an article in her college alumnae magazine, which reflected on the life of her mother. It caught the eye of an editor who asked her to consider writing a book about her childhood. Surprised but intrigued, Santiago did. *When I Was Puerto Rican* appeared to great praise in 1993. It was one of the first autobiographies of a Puerto Rican woman ever published in either English or Spanish.

Santiago followed up her success with a novel, *America's Dream*, in 1996. It is the story of a Puerto Rican woman escaping an abusive relationship. "I've been there," she told an audience at a women's shelter.[14] *Almost a Woman,* a sequel to *When I Was Puerto Rican,* was published in 1998. Santiago does the Spanish translations of her books herself and they have been best-sellers in Puerto Rico.

"I write for women," she declares. Although she does not intend to reflect badly on men, "my intention [is] to be . . . truthful."[15] Santiago is pleased to consider herself a role model. "I take my responsibility as a Puerto Rican woman very seriously," she says. "If I stumble, those behind me will fall. I want to stay upright so that those behind me can stand tall and proud."[16]

Gary Soto
(April 12, 1952–)

Gary Soto skimmed the shelves of the Fresno City College Library. He didn't really know what he was looking for. He didn't even particularly want to go to college, but he had enrolled to escape military service that would have sent him to fight in the Vietnam War. Still, he had always enjoyed reading, so when he saw a book titled *New American Poetry*, he pulled it from the shelf and flipped through it. He stopped at a poem by Edward Field called "Unwanted," and began to read. The poem had a titanic effect on the nineteen-year-old. That's "exactly how I felt at the time, unwanted," he remembers. Instantly, he decided, "Well, I'm going to try this, too."[1]

Gary Soto was born in Fresno, California, on April 12, 1952. His four grandparents had been born in

Gary Soto seeks out and publishes young Mexican-American writers in his Chicano Chapbooks series. "I want to replace myself," he says.

Mexico, but both his parents were American. Manuel Soto, his father, was born in California and Angie Treviño Soto, his mother, in Texas. Manuel Soto wanted his children to grow up American and decided that English was the language the family would speak at home. However, Gary spoke some Spanish to relatives who lived nearby, especially his grandmother.

Neither of Gary's parents had graduated from high school. Both worked long hours at very low-paying jobs to support their three children, Rick, Gary, and Debra. Manuel Soto worked at the Sunmaid Raisin Company and, Angie Soto peeled potatoes for a company called Redi-Spud. When Gary was only five, his father was killed in an industrial accident. The family plunged into poverty. Mrs. Soto was forced to work several jobs to keep their heads above water.

A few years later, she remarried and had another son, Jimmy. Her second husband was an Anglo, a hard drinker who often fought with his wife and stepchildren. Gary "stayed outside a lot" once his step-father moved in, he wrote. "It was scary to go inside."[2]

Gary found refuge at a nearby city playground. Always ready to swim, to play kickball or dodgeball, to make something in arts and crafts, he whiled away the hours from morning till night. "I was a fighter on occasion too," he admits, "a rambunctious kid."[3]

Though he liked to read, Gary was a poor student who daydreamed "all the time" in school, he says.[4] No one else in his family read or particularly valued education. At home, they only owned three books: a Catholic dictionary, a medical dictionary and a cookbook. Nor were his family's expectations for his future very high. He recalls his mother saying to him, "*M' ijo* (my son), if you don't go to prison, I will be proud of you."[5]

In high school, in spite of his lackluster academic performance, he did enjoy reading poetry in English classes.

At the end of his junior year, Gary ran away from home after an argument with his stepfather. He hitchhiked south and landed in Glendale, California. There, he found a job at a tire factory. The strenuous, filthy labor was even worse than the farmwork Gary had spent doing his previous summers. He returned home for his senior year.

Gary graduated from Fresno's Roosevelt High School with a 1.6, or high D, average in 1970. He promptly received a letter from the U.S. government ordering him to report for duty in the army. "Dumb, but not that dumb," he says, he took the easiest way out.[6] Full-time college students could not be drafted, so Soto enrolled in the closest and cheapest college he could find, Fresno City. He worked part-time to pay his expenses and lived at home.

Gary began keeping a journal and writing poems. His first attempts were crude, without correct spelling or grammar. But he persevered and also improved his grades enough to transfer to California State University at Fresno in 1972.

At Cal State, Gary took his first creative writing course. His teacher was Philip Levine, a well-known poet himself. Levine was "harsh" and could "make people cry," Soto says. But every semester he would "take a couple of clods in his classroom and would shape them into poets."[7]

Levine quickly spotted Gary's talent and motivation. He recommended him for a scholarship to a summer workshop for minority writers. At the conference, "something clicked in my brain," Soto remembers.[8] He began to write freely and well for the first time. The poems that eventually became his first book poured out of him.

For fifteen years, since the death of Manuel Soto, Gary's father, no one in the family had spoken of him. No pictures of his father were displayed, either. They were hidden in drawers. Gary was overcome creatively with a "flood of memory," he says. He knew "my subject would be my father" and others like him, Chicano field and factory workers.[9]

Despite his own and his family's expectation that he would marry a Chicana, Gary surprised himself by falling in love with a Japanese-American neighbor, Carolyn Oda. They were married the year after Gary's 1974 graduation with honors from Cal State. Carolyn Soto worked as a waitress while her new husband studied for a master's degree in fine arts (creative writing) at the University of California, Irvine. He received his degree in 1976. The Sotos' only child, Mariko, a daughter, was born two years later.

Soto exploded onto the national poetry scene with his first book, *The Elements of San Joaquin*, in 1977. Critics lavished it with praise and Soto won several awards and grants as a result. One prestigious fellowship, from the Guggenheim Foundation, allowed him and his family to travel and live in Mexico for a year. Soto also began teaching English at the University of California at Berkeley in 1979. He followed up this success with three more well-received poetry collections before changing direction.

"I didn't tire of poetry," he explains, "but I wanted to move to a thicker forest."[10] In *Living Up the Street* (1985), Soto wrote short autobiographical prose pieces exploring his days as a "playground kid," and as a teen filled with confusion and longing.[11] Soto continued his exploration of the past with three more volumes of memoirs: *Small Faces* in 1986; *Lesser Evils* in 1988; and *A Summer Life* in 1990.

A steady stream of letters from young Chicano fans of his autobiographical writings led Soto to another creative turning point. "I thought I might be able to make readers and writers out of this group," he says.[12] Soto decided to start writing for young people, with the intention of giving them books that would reflect their own lives. His collection of short stories for teens, *Baseball in April*, was published in 1990. Set in Fresno, each story focused on a happiness or heartache of growing up.

"I love telling stories," Soto says.[13] During the 1990s, he wrote eight picture books, nine novels, three short story collections, even a play for young people. He has also published three volumes of poems written especially for children and directed three short films based on his books.

From the start of his crusade to promote reading and writing in the Chicano community, Soto has reached out to students in schools and libraries. He is ready to try anything to excite audiences about reading. He has sung songs, acted in skits, even competed in sports and led a parade! "Literature can make a difference to a marginal kid," he believes.[14]

However, he has not abandoned his first passion, poetry for adults. During the 1990s, he has added four more poetry collections to his writing accomplishments, including *New and Selected Poems* in 1995, a finalist for the National Book Award. As a poet, Soto describes himself as "an imagist, one who tries to provide a really

After twenty years as a poet and memoirist, Gary Soto began to write for children and teens. "I love telling stories," he says.

stark, quick image." He adds, "I feel that a leaner poem is a better poem."[15]

Soto lives in Berkeley, California, with his family. Still rambunctious, he loves to travel and keep active. During his long days writing, he takes breaks to lift weights in the backyard. He plays basketball and holds a black belt in tae kwan do. As he nears his fifties, Soto continues to study various martial arts despite two bad knees. He does "low kicks and wimpy punches" he jokes.[16]

Although Soto resigned his Berkeley professorship in 1993, he returned to teaching in 1999. He was appointed Distinguished Professor of Creative Writing at the University of California at Riverside. Working at this campus is particularly appealing to him, since it is the most ethnically diverse in the UC system. His classes are open to all students, of course, but he especially seeks Latinos so that eventually he can "replace myself," he says.[17]

The turn of the century brought Soto new experiences and honors. He was one of five distinguished Latinos to receive the 1999 Hispanic Heritage Award. The black-tie ceremony was broadcast nationwide on television. His first novel for adults, *Nickel and Dime*, was published in 2000. It tells of the bumbling attempts at crime by two ex-security guards and a failed Chicano poet. No one, however, would make the mistake of thinking the novel autobiographical. The dynamic and driven Soto is anything but a failure.

Piri Thomas

(September 30, 1928–   )

Youth worker Piri Thomas met Richard Leacock, a filmmaker, when Leacock came to New York to shoot a documentary on street gangs in the early 1960s. The two men became friends and often talked together about Thomas's past as a drug addict and prison inmate. Leacock thought there might be a book in Thomas's experiences and offered to introduce him to an editor friend.[1]

In fact, Thomas already had an autobiographical manuscript, which he had begun writing in prison. He hurried home to get it, but it wasn't there. He asked his wife where the manuscript was. "Was that important?" she asked. Apparently, their children had played with it and so mussed its pages that she had thrown the entire thing into the incinerator. Tears overflowed Thomas's eyes as he realized that the only copy of his book was gone. "You wrote it

Piri Thomas

once," he told himself, trying to calm down, "You can write it again…only better."[2]

When Piri was born in New York on September 30, 1928, the name on his birth certificate was John Thomas, Jr. But that was an English version of his Cuban father's real name, Juan Tomas de la Cruz. His father let the "Yankee Doodle version" stand, Thomas says, in hopes that his son might have a "better chance of making it in America."[3] The whole family took the last name Thomas. Thomas's Puerto Rican mother, Dolores (Lola) Montañez, gave him the nickname Piri, which he later took as his legal name.

Piri was the oldest of his family's seven children, only four of whom would live to adulthood. The family lived in Manhattan's Spanish Harlem, or El Barrio, a predominantly Puerto Rican neighborhood. "We lived in three worlds," Thomas remembers, "home, school and the streets."[4]

The Thomas family was bilingual but spoke Spanish at home. They played games together, put on family shows, and listened to radio serials. On cold winter days, Doña Lola, as Piri's mother was called, served her children hot chocolate and warm them up with stories of her tropical childhood. She was "a fine storyteller," Thomas says.[5]

At public school Piri learned English. Though an indifferent student, Piri loved to read and remembers haunting the New York Public Library branch near his home. He always left the library "pregnant," he says.[6] He held the two books he was allowed to check out and several more under his jacket.

It was the third world, the street, that held the most allure and danger for the young man. Whenever he left their apartment, Doña Lola gave him her blessing, a Puerto Rican tradition, asking God to keep him safe. He needed it. By the time Piri was twelve, the group of Puerto Rican boys he ran with grew from a stickball team that stuck together for protection, into a gang. At this time, shortly before World War II, each ethnic group in the area, Puerto Rican, Irish, Italian, African American, had its own turf. They regularly brawled with their enemies. Piri was seriously injured in street fights.

In 1943, when Piri was fourteen, his father won a large amount of money gambling. Because he had also recently gotten a good job working in a factory that made airplanes for the war, Mr. Thomas used the windfall to buy a house in the suburbs. The family moved to Babylon, New York, on Long Island.

There, Piri found, he was "the only little coffee bean for miles around in a sea of white milk."[7] Like many Puerto Rican and Cuban families, the Thomases were racially mixed. Piri's siblings took after their light-skinned mother. Piri resembled his more dark-skinned father and was the family member who looked most African-American. His mother often affectionately called him *negrito*, or "little dark one." Though he was used to ethnic distinctions, having racial prejudice applied to him was something new to Piri. He quickly began to resent being spurned by girls at school dances and being asked if his sister was really his sister.

The conflict Piri felt over his family's racial identity grew. When his brother admitted that family members constantly made excuses for Piri's appearance to their neighbors, Piri exploded.[8] He quit school in tenth grade and returned to El Barrio in Manhattan alone. Essentially homeless, he bunked with various relatives and friends. Though he worked odd jobs, he began dabbling in drugs and petty crime. When his mother died of heart disease at age thirty-four, Thomas cut his ties with his family. A trip to the South with a black friend, during which a white driver wielding a gun forced Thomas to the back of the bus, hardened his anger. "I came back to New York with a big hate for anything white," he wrote.[9]

His downward spiral continued. He became addicted to heroin. Although he joined the merchant marine, between sea voyages he supported himself through petty crime. Finally, he took part in the armed robbery of a bar. In the gun battle that resulted, both he and a police officer were shot. When Thomas recovered, he was sent to prison, at age twenty-one, for fifteen years.

He spent his first two years in jail in "a gray mass of hatred," he says.[10] But slowly, he began to reflect on how he had come to this state. He felt shame for forgetting his mother's wisdom. "We all have powers in us," she often had told him. "One of them is of darkness and the other of light, and it's up to us to choose."[11]

The first choice Thomas made was to educate himself. He earned his high school diploma and for the first time in many years felt pride in his achievement. Then, he returned to his love of reading. Finally, he began to write "to find out who I was and where I came from," he says. He wrote about his childhood "to be with my family again." And he wrote to "overcome the rage" and keep himself from being a "walking time bomb."[12]

In 1957, after seven years in prison, Thomas was paroled and released in time for Christmas. He went to live with his mother's sister in Spanish Harlem and joined her Pentecostal church. There he found a loving community and met his future wife, Daniela Calo. Through the church, Thomas got a job counseling teenagers, gang members, and drug addicts with a social agency, Youth Development Incorporated. He married Calo in 1959 and they had two children, Ricardo and San-Dee.

Thomas had now escaped from the street. He had a settled life and a family of his own, but to rewrite his destroyed manuscript was to "open Pandora's box," he says. Feeling his rage again while writing was so wrenching, he would punch in walls. "But once I discovered that the truth brought relief from pain, it was wonderful," he adds.[13]

Thomas delivered the rewritten manuscript to Richard Leacock's friend, editor Angus Cameron of Knopf Publishers, who accepted it. When *Down These Mean Streets* appeared in 1967, it was the first book ever published by a Puerto Rican writer in English to be released by a major New York publisher. It became a best-seller and has stayed in print ever since. Over thirty years later, Thomas still meets fans who say it was the first book they ever read. Critic Humberto Cintron calls him "a legend in his community."[14]

Two documentary films about Piri Thomas's life were produced during the 1960s. *Petey and Johnny* (1961) and *The World of Piri Thomas* (1968). During the 1970s, Thomas wrote two sequels to his autobiography, *Savior, Savior, Hold My Hand* (1972), which described his life after prison, and *Seven Long Times* (1974), which covered his prison years. He had a play produced in New York by the Puerto Rican Traveling Theatre. To Thomas's satisfaction, his voting rights (lost when he was convicted of a felony) were restored by the governor of New York.

Thomas's first marriage ended in divorce. He then married Betty Gross, an attorney, and they moved to San Francisco in 1983. After his second wife died, he married Suzanne Dod, who had grown up in Puerto Rico as the child of Christian missionaries. He and his wife now live in El Cerrito, California.

For some years, Thomas has been refining a final volume for his autobiography, which he has titled *A Matter of Dignity*. He also writes poetry and performs it to Latin and New Age music. He has released two poetry CDs, *Sounds of the Streets* and *No Mo' Barrio Blues*. His current project is a documentary film about his work, called *Every Child Is Born a Poet*, directed by Jonathan Robinson.

Now in his seventies, Thomas often performs, lectures, and teaches writing at schools and colleges. But he still makes a point to meet with prison inmates. He has a special message for them. "[I tell them] not to serve time, but to have time serve them," he says. "To educate their mind, not to eradicate it."[15] He is the living example of what they can do. "I ain't saying nothing to them that I . . . read in a book," he says. "I am saying what I have lived. I *am* a book."[16]

"We lived in three worlds," Piri Thomas says of his family. "Home, school, and the streets" of Manhattan's Spanish Harlem. Piri is at the left.

Further Reading
and Selected Bibliography
(with Internet Addresses)

Augenbaum, Harold, ed. *Growing Up Latino: Memoirs and Stories.* Boston: Houghton Mifflin, 1993.

Bruce-Novoa, Juan D. *Chicano Authors: Inquiry by Interview.* Austin, Tex.: University of Texas Press, 1980.

Hernandez, Carmen Dolores. *Puerto Rican Voices in English: Interviews with Writers.* Westport, Conn.: Praeger, 1997.

Sullivan, Charles, ed. *Here is My Kingdom: Hispanic-American Literature and Art for Young People.* New York: Harry N. Abrams, 1994.

Internet Addresses

"Voices from the Gaps: Women Writers of Color," <http://voices.cla.umn.edu>.

"A Casa of My Own," webcast of a speech by Judith Ortiz Cofer <www.education.wisc.edu/ccbc/webcast.htm>

"Gary Soto's Homepage," <www.garysoto.com>

"Piri Thomas's Homepage," <www.cheverote. com>

By Julia Alvarez

For adults

Homecoming, 1984
How the Garcia Girls Lost Their Accents, 1991
In the Time of the Butterflies, 1994
The Other Side/El Otro Lado, 1995
Yo!, 1996
In the Name of Salome, 2000

For young people
Tia Lola Stories, 2000

About Julia Alvarez
Alvarez, Julia. *Something to Declare*. New York: Plume, 1998.
Contemporary Authors, New Revision Series, Vol. 69. Detroit: Gale, 1999.

By Rudolfo Anaya

For adults
Bless Me, Ultima, 1972
Heart of Atzlán, 1976
Tortuga, 1979
A Chicano in China, 1986
Alburquerque, 1992
Zia Summer, 1995
Rio Grande Fall, 1996
Shaman Winter, 1999

For young people
The Farolitos of Christmas, 1997

About Rudolfo Anaya
Contemporary Authors, Autobiography Series, Vol. 4. Detroit, Gale, 1990.
Contemporary Authors, New Revision Series, Vol. 51. Detroit: Gale, 1996.
Fernandez Olmos, Margarite. *Rudolfo A. Anaya: A Critical Companion*. Westport, Conn.: Greenwood Press, 1999.

By Sandra Cisneros

For adults
The House on Mango Street, 1984
My Wicked, Wicked Ways, 1987
Woman Hollering Creek, 1991

Loose Woman, 1994

About Sandra Cisneros

Mirriam-Goldberg, Caryn. *Sandra Cisneros: Latina Writer and Activist.* Berkeley Heights, N.J.: Enslow, 1998.

Contemporary Authors, New Revision Series, Vol. 64. Detroit: Gale, 1998.

By Judith Ortiz Cofer

For adults

Terms of Survival, 1987
The Line of the Sun, 1989
The Latin Deli, 1993

For young people

An Island Like You: Stories of the Barrio, 1995
The Year of Our Revolution, 1998

About Judith Ortiz Cofer

Cofer, Judith Ortiz. *Silent Dancing: A Partial Remembrance of a Puerto Rican Childhood.* Houston, Tx.: Arte Publico, 1990.

Contemporary Authors, New Revision Series, V. 72. Detroit: Gale, 1999.

By Oscar Hijuelos

For adults

Our House in the Last World, 1983
The Mambo Kings Play Songs of Love, 1989
The Fourteen Sister of Emilio Montez O'Brien, 1993
Mr. Ives' Christmas, 1995
Empress of the Splendid Season, 1999

About Oscar Hijuelos

Hijuelos, Oscar. "Introduction." *Cool Salsa: Bilingual Poems on Growing Up Latino in the United States.* New York: Henry Holt, 1994.

Contemporary Authors, New Revision Series, Vol. 75. Detroit: Gale, 2000.

By Nicholasa Mohr

For adults

Rituals of Survival, 1985

A Matter of Pride and Other Stories, 1997

For young people

Nilda, 1973

El Bronx Remembered, 1975

In Nueva York, 1977

Felita, 1979

Going Home, 1986

The Magic Shell, 1995

About Nicholasa Mohr

Something About the Author: Autobiography Series, Vol. 8. Detroit: Gale, 1989.

Mohr, Nicholasa. *In My Own Words: Growing Up Inside the Sanctuary of My Imagination.* New York: Julian Messner, 1994.

Contemporary Authors, New Revision Series, Vol. 64. Detroit: Gale, 1998.

By Richard Rodriguez

Days of Obligation: An Argument with My Mexican Father, 1992.

About Richard Rodriguez

Rodriguez, Richard. *The Hunger of Memory: The Education of Richard Rodriguez.* New York: Bantam, 1982.

Contemporary Authors, New Revision Series, Vol. 66. Detroit: Gale, 1998.

By Esmeralda Santiago

For adults

America's Dream, 1996

Las Christmas: Favorite Latino Authors Share Their Holiday Memories, 1998

Las Mamis: Favorite Latino Authors Remember Their Mothers, 2000

About Esmeralda Santiago

Santiago, Esmeralda. *Almost a Woman.* Reading, Mass.: Perseus, 1998.

Santiago, Esmeralda. *When I Was Puerto Rican.* Reading, Mass.: Addison-Wesley, 1993.

Contemporary Authors, Vol. 179. Detroit: Gale, 2000.

By Gary Soto

For adults

The Elements of San Joaquin, 1977

The Tale of Sunlight, 1978

Where Sparrows Work Hard, 1981

Black Hair, 1985

Who Will Know Us?, 1990

Home Course in Religion, 1991

Local News, 1993

New and Selected Poems, 1995

Junior College, 1997

A Natural Man, 1999

Nickel and Dime, 2000

For young people

Baseball in April and Other Stories, 1990

A Fire in My Hands, 1990

Jesse, 1994

Chato's Kitchen, 1995

Buried Onions, 1997

About Gary Soto

Soto, Gary. *Living Up the Street.* San Francisco: Strawberry Hill, 1985.

Soto, Gary. *Small Faces.* Houston, Tx.: Arte Publico, 1986.

Soto, Gary. *Lesser Evils.* Houston, Tx.: Arte Publico, 1988.

Soto, Gary. *A Summer Life.* New York: Dell, 1990.

Contemporary Authors, New Revision Series, V. 74. Detroit: Gale, 1999.

Hill, Christine M. *Ten Terrific Authors for Teens.* Berkeley Heights, N.J.: Enslow, 2000.

By Piri Thomas

For young people

Stories of El Barrio, 1978

About Piri Thomas

Thomas, Piri. *Down These Mean Streets.* New York: Knopf, 1967.

Thomas, Piri. *Savior, Savior, Hold My Hand.* New York: Doubleday, 1972.

Thomas, Piri. *Seven Long Times.* Houston, Tex.: Arte Publico, 1994.

Contemporary Authors, Vols. 73–76. Detroit: Gale, 1978.

Chapter Notes

Preface

1. Jonathan Bing, "Julia Alvarez: Books That Cross Borders," *Publishers Weekly*, December 16, 1996, p. 39.

2. Rafael Ocasio, "An Interview with Judith Ortiz Cofer," *Americas Review*, Fall/Winter 1994, p. 86.

3. Humberto Cintron, "An Interview with Piri Thomas," <www.cheverote.com/reviews/cintroninterview.html> (September, 14, 2001).

4. Linda Robinson, "Hispanics Don't Exist," *U.S. News and World Report*, May 11, 1998, p. 27.

5. Ibid.

Chapter 1. Julia Alvarez

1. Julia Alvarez, *Something to Declare* (New York: Plume, 1998), p. 139.

2. *Contemporary Authors* (Detroit: Gale, 1999) vol. 69, p. 8.

3. Alvarez, p. 140.

4. *Contemporary Authors*, p. 8.

5. Jonathan Bing, "Julia Alvarez: Books That Cross Borders," *Publishers Weekly*, December 16, 1996, p. 39.

6. Heather Rosario-Sievert, "Conversation with Julia Alvarez," *Review: Latin American Literature and Arts*, vol. 54, Spring 1997, p. 32.

7. Marny Requa, "Julia Alvarez: The Politics of Fiction," <www.fronteramag.com> See Table of Contents/Site Index, Issue 5, *Julia Alvarez.* (September 14, 2001).

8. *Contemporary Authors*, p. 8.

9. Bing, p. 39.

10. Alvarez, p. 221.

11. Ibid., p. 142.

12. Requa, "Julia Alvarez."

13. Bing, p. 39.

14. Letter to the author, June 17, 2000.

15. Alvarez, p. 111.

16. Rosario-Sievert, p. 36.

Chapter 2. Rudolfo Anaya

1. Juan D. Bruce-Novoa, *Chicano Authors: Inquiry by Interview* (Austin: University of Texas Press), 1980, p. 185.

2. Ibid., p. 184.

3. *Contemporary Authors: Autobiography Series* (Detroit: Gale, 1995), vol. 4, p. 17.

4. Bruce-Novoa, p. 188.

5. Paul Vassallo, ed., *The Magic of Words: Rudolfo A. Anaya and His Writings* (Albuquerque: University of New Mexico Press), 1982, p. 10.

6. Ibid., p. 11.

7. *Contemporary Authors: Autobiography Series*, p. 17.

8. Vassallo, p. 14.

9. *Contemporary Authors: Autobiography Series*, p. 20.

10. Ibid., p. 21.

11. William Clark, "Rudolfo Anaya: The Chicano Worldview," *Publishers Weekly*, June 5, 1995, p. 42.

12. *Contemporary Authors: Autobiography Series*, p. 23.

13. Ibid.

14. Clark, p. 41.

15. Ibid.

16. R.S. Sharma, "Interview With Rudolfo Anaya," *Prairie Schooner*, Winter 1994, p. 186.

17. Clark, p. 42.

Chapter 3. Sandra Cisneros

1. Robin Ganz, "Sandra Cisneros: Border Crossings and Beyond," *Melus*, Spring 1994. p. 23.

2. Jim Sagel, "Sandra Cisneros," *Publishers Weekly*, March 29, 1991, p. 75.

3. Ibid.

4. Sandra Cisneros, "Ghosts and Voices: Writing from Obsession," *Americas Review*, Spring 1987, p. 69.

5. Sagel, p. 74.

6. Raul Nino, "The Booklist Interview: Sandra Cisneros," *Booklist*, September 1, 1993, p. 36.

7. Ganz, p. 27.

8. Kelli Pryor, "Close Up: Sandra Cisneros," *Entertainment Weekly*, April 26, 1991, p. 11.

9. Feroza Jussawalla, *Interviews with Writers of the Post-Colonial World* (Jackson: University Press of Mississippi), p. 302.

10. Ibid., p. 301.

11. Pilar E. Rodriguez Aranda, "On the Solitary Fate of Being Mexican, Female, Wicked and Thirty-Three: An Interview with Writer Sandra Cisneros," *Americas Review*, Spring 1990, p. 74.

12. Jussawalla, p. 305.

13. Letter to the author, June 21, 2000.

14. Sagel, p. 75.

15. Martha Satz, "Returning to One's House: An Interview with Sandra Cisneros," *Southwest Review*, Spring 1997, p. 170.

16. Ibid., p. 181.

17. Letter to the author, June 21, 2000.

18. Satz, p.166.

19. Sandra Cisneros, "Heritage: An Offering to the Power of Language," *Los Angeles Times*, October 26, 1997, Opinion p. 1.

Chapter 4. Judith Ortiz Cofer

1. Rafael Ocasio, "An Interview With Judith Ortiz Cofer," *Americas Review*, Fall/Winter 1994, p. 84.

2. Judith Ortiz Cofer, *The Latin Deli* (New York: Norton, 1993), p. 131.

3. Rafael Ocasio, "Puerto Rican Literature in Georgia: An Interview with Judith Ortiz Cofer," *Kenyon Review*, Fall 1992, p. 43.

4. Carmen D. Hernandez, *Puerto Rican Voices in English: Interviews with Writers* (Westport, Conn.: Praeger, 1997), p. 101.

5. Ocasio, *Americas Review*, p. 87.

6. Paul Karr, "The Quilting of Cultures," *University of Georgia Research Reporter*, Fall 1998, p. 17.

7. Cofer, p. 127.

8. Judith Ortiz Cofer, *Silent Dancing: A Partial Remembrance of a Puerto Rican Childhood* (Houston: Arte Publico, 1990), p. 143.

9. Hernandez, p. 99.

10. Edna Acosta-Belen, "A Melus Interview: Judith Ortiz Cofer," *Melus*, Fall 1993, p. 91.

11. Karr, p. 18.

12. Hernandez, p. 102.

13. Rafael Ocasio, "Speaking in Puerto Rican: An Interview with Judith Ortiz Cofer," *Bilingual Review*, May-August 1992, p. 144.

14. Ocasio, *Americas Review*, p. 86.

15. Ibid., p. 87.

Chapter 5. Oscar Hijuelos

1. Lydia Chaves, "Cuban Riffs and Songs of Love," *Los Angeles Times Magazine*, April 18, 1993, p. 24.

2. Michael Coffey, "Oscar Hijuelos," *Publishers' Weekly*, July 21, 1989, p. 44.

3. Lori M. Carlson, ed. *Cool Salsa: Bilingual Poems on Growing Up Latino in the United States* (New York: Holt, 1994), p. xviii.

4. Ibid.

5. Ibid., p. xvi.

6. Chaves, p. 24.

7. Carlson, p. xviii.

8. Dinitia Smith, "Sisters'Act," *New York*, March 1, 1993, pp. 50–51.

9. "Chat Transcripts: Oscar Hijuelos," February 4, 1999, <www.barnesandnoble.com/community/a...ZN3K0017QU6 AL47QA7V8&srefer=&eventId=1394> (September 14, 2001).

10. Ibid.

11. Esther B.Fein, "Oscar Hijuelos's Unease, Wordly and Otherwise," *New York Times*, April 1, 1993, p. C17.

12. Chaves, p. 25.

13. Smith, pp. 50–51.

14. "Chat Transcripts."

Chapter 6. Nicholasa Mohr

1. Nicholasa Mohr, *In My Own Words: Growing Up Inside the Sanctuary of My Imagination* (New York: Julian Messner, 1994), p. 110.

2. *Something About the Author: Autobiography Series* (Detroit: Gale, 1989), vol. 8, p. 188.

3. Mohr, p. 14.

4. Carmen D. Hernandez, *Puerto Rican Voices in English: Interviews with Writers* (Westport, Conn.: Praeger, 1997), p. 88.

5. Mohr, p. 10.

6. *Something About the Author*, p. 185.

7. Mohr, p. 78.

8. Ibid., p. 104.

9. *Something About the Author*, p. 189.

10. Ibid., p. 192.

11. Myra Zarnowski, "An Interview with Author Nicholasa Mohr," *Reading Teacher*, October 1991, p. 104.

12. "Profiles: Contemporary Writers, Nicholasa Mohr," *Heath Anthology of American Literature Online*, Fall 1992 <www.georgetown.edu/tamlit/ newsletter/numb8tex.html>.

13. Hernandez, p. 87.

14. Eneid Routte-Gomez, "Rituals of Survival—Women Coping with Fear," *San Juan Star*, July 29, 1985, p. 5

15. Zarnowski, p. 103.

Chapter 7. Richard Rodriguez

1. Richard Rodriguez, *The Hunger of Memory: The Education of Richard Rodriguez* (New York: Bantam, 1982), p. 20.

2. Ibid., p. 21.

3. Richard Rodriguez, "Going Home Again: The New American Scholarship Boy," *American Scholar*, Winter 1974, p. 17.

4. Elizabeth Sherwin, "Rodriguez Remembers Sacramento in His Books," <www.davis.ca.us/go/gizmo/1997/rr1.htm/> (September 14, 2001).

5. Rodriguez, *The Hunger of Memory*, p. 61.

6. Rodriguez, "Going Home Again," p. 20.

7. Ibid., p. 21.

8. Timothy Sedore, "Violating the Boundaries: An Interview with Richard Rodriguez," *Michigan Quarterly Review,* Summer 1999, p. 427.

9. Rodriguez, p. 23.

10. Rodriguez, *The Hunger of Memory,* p. 171.

11. Patricia Holt, "Richard Rodriguez," *Publishers Weekly,* March 26, 1982, p. 7.

12. Scott London, "Crossing Borders: An Interview with Richard Rodriguez," *The Sun Magazine,* August 1997 <www.west.net/~insight/rr. htm> (September 14, 2001).

13. Holt, p. 6.

14. Sedore, p. 433.

15. Ibid., p. 445.

16. Paul Crowley, "An Ancient Catholic: An Interview with Richard Rodriguez," *America,* September 23, 1995, p. 11.

17. Ibid., p. 9.

18. London, "Crossing Borders."

19. Postrel, Virginia. "The New, New World: Richard Rodriguez on Culture and Assimilation," *Reason,* August 5, 1994, p. 36.

Chapter 8. Esmeralda Santiago

1. Carmen D. Hernandez, *Puerto Rican Voices in English* (Westport, Conn.: Praeger, 1997), p. 162.

2. "Esmeralda Santiago," *The Reading Group Center,* <www.randomhouse.com/vintage/read/puerto/santiago. html> (September 14, 2001).

3. Esmeralda Santiago, *When I Was Puerto Rican* (Reading, Mass.: Addison-Wesley, 1993), p. 209.

4. Esmeralda Santiago, *Almost a Woman* (New York: Vintage, 1998), p. 17.

5. John Koch, "Esmeralda Santiago," *Boston Globe Magazine,* September 20, 1998, <www.boston.com/globe/magazine/9-20/interview/> (September 14, 2001).

6. Esmeralda Santiago, "Mami: Paying Her Own Way," *Radcliffe Quarterly,* June 1990, pp. 29–30.

7. Santiago, *When I Was Puerto Rican*, p. 259.

8. Santiago, *Almost a Woman*, p. 74.

9. Koch, "Esmeralda Santiago."

10. Sharon Egiebor, "Author Speaks from Experience About Escaping Emotional Abuse," *Dallas Morning News*, June 12, 1996, p. 5c.

11. Esmeralda Santiago, "At 26 a New Beginning," *Radcliffe Quarterly*, June 1975, p. 38.

12. Koch, "Esmeralda Santiago."

13. Hernandez, p. 165.

14. Egiebor, "Author Speaks from Experience."

15. Hernandez, pp. 160–161.

16. Noelani Schneider, "Santiago Opens Women's Month With 'the Unspoken'," *Brown Daily Herald*, March 4, 1997, <www.thehearald.org/issues/030497/convocation.f.html> (September 14, 2001).

Chapter 9. Gary Soto

1. Joseph Parisi, *Poets in Person*. [audiotape] (Chicago: Modern Poetry Association, 1991).

2. Gary Soto, *A Summer Life* (New York: Dell, 1990), p. 105.

3. Jeffrey Copeland, *Speaking of Poets: Interviews with Poets Who Write for Children and Young Adults* (Urbana, Ill.: National Council of Teachers of English, 1993), p.91.

4. "Authors Online: Gary Soto,"<www2.scholastic.com/teachers/authorsandbooks/authorstudies/authorstudies.jhtml?IndexLetter=S> See Interview Transcript. (September 14, 2001)

5. Parisi, *Poets in Person*.

6. Ibid.

7. Wolfgang Binder, *Partial Autobiographies: Interviews with Twenty Chicano Poets* (Erlangen, Germany: Verlag Palm & Enke, 1985), p. 192.

8. Ibid., p. 193.

9. Parisi, *Poets in Person*.

10. "Gary Soto," *Hispanic American Biography* (New York: UXL, 1995), vol. 2, p. 215.

11. Copeland, p. 91.

12. Don Lee, "About Gary Soto," *Ploughshares,* Spring 1995, p. 188.

13. Copeland, p. 94.

14. *Hispanic American Biography,* p. 215.

15. Copeland, p. 91.

16. Soto, p. 82.

17. "New UCR Poet Writes for NASA, Misses Launch," <www.ucr.edu/SubPages/2CurNewsFold/UnivRelat/soto2.html> (September 14, 2001).

Chapter 10. Piri Thomas

1. Carmen D. Hernandez, *Puerto Rican Voices in English* (Westport, Conn.: Praeger, 1997), p. 179.

2. Humberto Cintron, "An Interview with Piri Thomas," <www.cheverote.com/reviews/cintroninterview.html> (September 14, 2001).

3. Hernandez, p. 173.

4. Cintron, "Piri Thomas."

5. Nic Paget-Clarke, "Interview with Piri Thomas," *In Motion Magazine,* <www.inmotionmagazine.com/ptinter1.html> (September 14, 2001).

6. Hernandez, p. 176.

7. Ilan Stavans, "Race and Mercy: A Conversation with Piri Thomas," *Massachusetts Review,* Autumn 1996.

8. Piri Thomas, *Down These Mean Streets* (New York: Knopf, 1967), p. 146.

9. Ibid., p. 195.

10. Ibid., p. 256.

11. Cintron, "Piri Thomas."

12. Ibid.

13. Stavans, p. .

14. Cintron, "Piri Thomas."

15. Letter to the author, June 14, 2000.

16. Paget-Clarke, "Piri Thomas."

Index

111